D1627901

DreamWorks

Trolls

POPPY and the Parade Problem

Scholastic Children's Books,
Euston House, 24 Eversholt Street,
London NW1 1DB, UK

A division of Scholastic Ltd
London ~ New York ~ Toronto ~ Sydney ~ Auckland
Mexico City ~ New Delhi ~ Hong Kong

First published in Australia by Bonnier Publishing, 2017, as two titles:
Poppy and the Parade Problem
Biggie and the Big Mix-Up
This edition published in the UK by Scholastic Ltd, 2018

Poppy and the Parade Problem written by Katie Hewat
Biggie and the Big Mix-Up written by Fiona Harris

ISBN 978 1407 17140 1

Printed and bound in the UK by CPI (Group) Ltd, Croydon, Surrey

2 4 6 8 10 9 7 5 3 1

Papers used by Scholastic Children's Books are made from wood grown in
sustainable forests.

www.scholastic.co.uk

POPPY and the Parade Problem

📖 SCHOLASTIC

Chapter 1

Queen Poppy feels certain that today is going to be the happiest, singing-est, dancing-est, most hug-filled day in the history of Troll Village!

Every day is her favourite day, because Poppy believes you never can have a better day than the one that is happening right now.

Poppy is one seriously happy Troll.

With her bubbly, positive attitude, Queen Poppy inspires other Trolls to feel happy, too.

Poppy swings out of her pod just in time to catch the Caterbus! She leaps aboard and sinks into the critter's soft felt fur. As it marches quickly towards the centre of the village, Poppy waves to groups of singing, dancing, hugging Trolls who stop to wave back at their queen. Even this early in the morning, Troll Village is buzzing.

It's not long before Poppy spots her friends at one of their popular hang-outs. She jumps off the Caterbus and runs towards them.

Cooper sees Poppy first. He is lying on a spongy patch of grassy felt filled with fuzzy rainbow-coloured flowers.

'Poppy!' he squeals, leaping to his feet. 'Sing with me!' They launch into one of their favourite tunes and Cooper busts some wicked dance moves.

No Troll can resist a good singalong. DJ Suki hops on her Wooferbug and starts mixing a bouncing beat. Soon Biggie, Smidge, Guy Diamond, Harper and Satin and Chenille are all joining in. Only Branch is sitting aside, looking sheepish. Oh, Branch!

As the song ends, Satin and Chenille sling Poppy high into the air with their colourful connected hair. Poppy somersaults up and over, coming to land in a *Ta-da!*-like pose beside Branch.

He gives her a *you're-so-crazy* eye-roll. Poppy plonks down beside him, reaches into her hair and pulls out her scrapbook. She snip-snips, dab-dabs, stick-sticks, whipping up a dazzling scene that records her morning so far.

Once she's finished, Poppy pulls her cowbell out of her hair. She bangs the bell to get everyone's attention.

'As you all know,' she begins, 'King Peppy's birthday is coming up, so I have decided to throw the most aaah-mazing, Troll-tastic surprise birthday parade ever!' Her friends cheer. Everyone knows Trolls love a good parade.

'Where are you going to have the parade?' asks Cooper.

'What are we going to wear?' ask Satin and Chenille.

'How are you going to make it the best parade ever, Queen Poppy?' asks Biggie.

Poppy scratches her head and looks around for inspiration but nothing comes to mind. 'Uh ... hmm ... I'm not really sure yet,' she mumbles. Every pair of eyes is on her, waiting for her to produce one of her famous grand plans, but she has nothing. Nada. Zilch-o. 'Let me get back to you,' she tells them.

Suddenly Poppy feels a little less like her usual confident self. 'Shouldn't a leader have the answers?' she wonders.

Later, as Poppy passes by Guy Diamond's dance studio, Guy comes out to greet Poppy. She can see he is so excited that glitter is actually bursting off him in little puffs.

7

'I've got the best idea ever!' he says.
'Let me choreograph a totally dance-a-rific parade. We'll get the whole village dancing together as one ... it will be like nothing King Peppy has ever seen before!'

Poppy hugs Guy. 'I love, love, love that idea,' she says, happy to have a solution.

A few minutes later, as Poppy is bopping along to a pulsing beat coming from a nearby pod, Harper leaps out in front of her. Harper's hair flicks from side to side, coating everything around her with bright splotches of paint.

'Poppy, I'm so glad I found you!' Harper gasps. 'I know what we have to do to make tomorrow's parade the best Troll Village has ever seen. Let me create giant papier mâché puppets of King Peppy that we can

parade through the village like a
moving art gallery.'

Poppy squeals and clasps her hands together. 'What a fabulous parade that would be!' she tells Harper.

Harper skips away, delighted, painting the village rainbow as she goes.

At first, Poppy feels relieved. She has two ideas that are just perfect!

But then she thinks, *Oh no! Two perfect ideas! But there is only one parade.*

How can she choose between two perfect ideas? To make matters worse if she chooses Guy Diamond's idea she will let Harper down.

If she chooses Harper's idea she will disappoint Guy Diamond. Choosing who to let down is even worse than choosing between two perfect ideas and the parade is tomorrow. What will she do?

Chapter 2

As the day goes on, Poppy's tummy is all twisted in a tight knot over the decision she has to make. She knows everyone would love a dance-a-thon, but a moving gallery would be so cool and unique, too.

She plonks down on a nearby log, startling a bunch of fuzzy butterflies into the air. On the other side of the clearing, she can see that two young

Trolls have managed to get their hair all tangled together during a hearty game of jump rope.

'You silly boy, your hair is all tangled in mine,' says the blue-haired Troll, pulling her head backwards to try and get her hair free.

'No, you're silly!' giggles the green-haired Troll. 'You got *your* hair stuck in *mine!*' he says as he yanks his own head backwards.

Poppy jumps up to help, but before she can take a step, her father has arrived on the scene. He sets about untangling the young Trolls' hair, while making

them giggle with a silly joke as he works away. Sure enough, he's soon sorted the problem and the happy little Trolls are hugging and laughing and playing once more.

Poppy sighs. *My father always knows exactly what to do in any situation,* she thinks to herself. She wishes she could go to him for advice about her problem, but that would spoil the surprise.

Poppy hears someone calling her name and looks up to see Guy swinging by his hair on a branch in a nearby tree. 'Can't wait for the parade!' he shouts down. He stretches his hair to lower himself from the tree.

Poppy waves a little sheepishly – what if she ends up choosing Harper's idea and has to let Guy down?

'This is going to be the most glitter-tastic dance routine EVER!' sings Guy in his autotune voice. 'I've dropped everything else to work on it! Have a glitter day!' he says, leaving a trail of glitter in his excitement as he uses his hair to swing off again.

Poppy plants her face in her hands. Guy has dropped everything to work on the dance routine – she can't say no to him now. She will have to talk to Harper.

When Poppy looks up, Branch is standing in front of her. His head is tilted to the side and he is looking very puzzled.

'I know I'm just getting the hang of this positivity thing,' he says, 'but I'm pretty sure your scrunched up face means you're not feeling positive right now.'

Poppy groans and tells him her problem. 'I have to choose between

two perfect parade ideas and let one of my friends down. And to make matters worse, I don't even have a single idea for a special gift to give my father for his birthday,' she says.

'Hmm,' Branch says and sits down beside her. He's deep in thought for a moment before he jerks his head up as if he's got an idea, then his shoulders sag. 'No ... that won't work,' he mumbles.

All of a sudden he leaps off the log. 'That's it!' he says. 'I have the perfect solution!' Poppy leaps up too and grabs his arms.

'What is it?' she asks. She's so relieved there is a solution!

'Well, for a gift, that's easy. How about a lock, a trap or an intruder alarm?' He reaches into his hair with both hands and rummages around, producing one of each item.

When Poppy doesn't respond Branch coughs quietly and puts them away, then lights up again. 'And as for the parade problem ... this is the best idea ever ... wait for it: just pick the idea you like the most!' he says, looking triumphant. Poppy can tell he's pretty pleased with himself right now.

'That is no help whatsoever, Branch!' she says and flops back down.

Branch looks puzzled again. He shrugs his shoulders. 'Well I'm sure you'll find a better solution yourself then, *your highness*,' he mutters as he stomps off.

I really have made a mess of things today, haven't I? Poppy thinks.

Chapter 3

Just when Poppy thinks matters can't get any worse, here comes Harper. Harper looks around to make sure no one else is watching, then reaches into her hair and pulls out three miniature papier mâché puppets. 'Mini samples!' she whispers excitedly, then gives Poppy the thumbs up and rushes off.

What in the world am I going to do? thinks Poppy. *Both of my friends have already*

started on their perfectly perfect ideas. How can I choose now?

Poppy makes up her mind to follow a piece of advice her father once gave her: a problem shared is a problem halved. Surely one of her other friends will be able to give her some good advice?

She decides to go and see Biggie. He is one of the kindest Trolls Poppy knows, after all. She is sure he'll understand why she doesn't want to hurt anyone's feelings. She finds Biggie sitting outside the cupcakery, clutching a basketful of assorted cupcakes.

When Poppy plops down next to him he smiles. She tells Biggie all about her problem. 'I love, love, love both Guy's and Harper's parade ideas, but I really don't want to hurt anyone's feelings,' she explains.

Biggie nods. Then his eyes fill with tears and he lets out a huge sob! He grabs a sparkle-frosted cupcake and shoves it in Poppy's mouth. 'Quickly, eat this,' he sobs. 'It's made from happy tears. It will make you feel better!' He gulps down another cupcake himself and immediately stops crying.

'Thanks,' Poppy says around a mouthful of cupcake. It does make her feel better, but only for a moment. 'What am I going to do about my problem, though?'

Biggie bursts into tears again. Poppy reaches over and passes him another happy-tears cupcake and gives him a big hug. She realizes cupcakes won't solve this problem – she needs advice.

As Poppy says goodbye to Biggie she notices Cooper inside the cupcakery.

Maybe Cooper can help? she wonders. Poppy finds Cooper working away on some delicious-looking treats.

She asks for his advice and he says he is more than happy to help. Poppy tells him she is having trouble choosing between two of their friends and their parade ideas.

'Guy has suggested a choreographed dance parade,' she tells him.

Cooper jumps up and down. 'Yes, we should definitely have a dance parade!' he says, and does a little moonwalk on the spot.

'But Harper wants to create a moving art gallery with giant puppets,' says Poppy.

Cooper's eyes widen. He claps his two

front feet together and wriggles his body. 'Oh, we should definitely have a puppet parade!' he cries.

'But with treats and presents and dancing and singing and hugging and glitter cannons, there will only be time for one parade,' Poppy reminds him. 'Which one would you choose?'

Cooper thinks for a moment. 'Oh, no, I couldn't possibly choose between them,' he says. Poppy's heart sinks. But she is grateful he understood her parade problem, at least.

Next, Poppy decides to visit Cybil. She's outside her pod, floating with

the help of a winged critter, with her legs crossed and her eyes closed, surely meditating one of life's great mysteries.

Poppy calls up to Cybil and she gently floats down to the ground. Cybil is a great friend, and Poppy just knows she'll have some wise advice to give.

Poppy tells Cybil all about her problem. When Poppy is finished Cybil tells her she will meditate on the issue. Poppy waits patiently while she does so.

Cybil soon opens her eyes. 'I know where the answer to your problem lies,' she says.

31

Finally! A solution. What a relief! thinks Poppy. She can feel the weight lifting from her shoulders already. 'Where?' she asks.

Cybil replies, 'You will find the answer within yourself.'

Poppy feels the weight of a Bergen settle squarely back onto her shoulders.

Chapter 4

A few hours later, Poppy is sitting beside the lake watching Glitter Falls cascade down the cliff face across from her. The falls send up a gentle cloud of glitter as they hit the shimmering surface of the lake.

Poppy lets out a deep sigh and absent-mindedly tosses bubblegum-berries into the lake. Poor Poppy. Her parade problem has left her not feeling herself.

Typically THE most positive Troll in Troll Village, she doesn't feel positive, bubbly or confident at all.

Usually this is her favourite place in Troll Village, but today she is hiding out to avoid running into Guy or Harper. She is actually starting to doubt herself – if she can't decide on a theme how will she lead the Trolls in tomorrow's parade? In fact how will she be a leader at all?

She simply must figure out a way to decide – Harper's awesome puppets or Guy's amazing dance routine? She watches glumly as sparkly fish leap up to gobble the berries.

Then she remembers. Scrapbooking! Scrapbooking always makes her happy. She even wonders if maybe she can scrapbook her way out of the situation!

As far as Poppy can see, she has two ways to solve her problem: 1. let Harper down and 2. let Guy down. Poppy would never hurt her friends' feelings. Oh dear!

She decides to create a scrapbook page for each scenario and see if that helps. She roots around in her hair until she finds everything she needs.

For the first page, she cuts out felt puppet shapes and layers blue on blue on blue. And not a happy kind of blue like the sky or her favourite flowered headband. This blue is a definite shade of despair.

Poppy feels it's just about perfect. *No, wait, it needs more sad face,* she thinks. 'There,' she says adding tears to the puppets. 'That's about right. That's the exact level of sorrow that will appear on Harper's face when I break the news to her.'

She begins working on the opposite page. This one she makes grey. 'Let's call this particular shade *crushed dreams*

grey,' she says to herself as she glues grey dancing Trolls to the page. 'And no glitter here. Glitter doesn't belong on this page. Nope, no glitter at all for Guy once I tell him the bad news.'

Poppy is feeling more hopeless than ever when she hears rustling behind her. She turns to see Branch coming down the path. 'I thought I'd find you here,' he says.

'I'm hiding,' she tells him. 'At least while I'm here nobody will find out I'm a terrible Troll, a bad leader and the worst friend ever.'

Branch sits down beside her. 'You're a great leader, Poppy, and the best kind of friend to every Troll in this village,' he says shyly. 'But sometimes it is really hard to make everyone happy ... even for you.'

Branch's words trigger something inside Poppy and she realises she has been looking at this the wrong way. She has been wondering how she could possibly disappoint one of her friends, when she should have been working out how to make everyone happy. She grins at Branch, feeling her bubbly and positive outlook return.

All of a sudden it feels like anything is possible!

She grabs her scrapbook, noticing that the glue hasn't quite dried yet. Poppy has an idea! She picks it up and closes it firmly.

When she opens it again, the two pages she has just created have melded together. There's now a mixture of colour on both pages. Some of the dancing Trolls have stuck to Harper's page and some of the puppets have stuck to Guy's page. She shakes glitter over the whole scene until it's totally glitterific!

41

Poppy laughs and gives Branch a huge hug.

'You're the best!' she calls over her shoulder as she starts running back towards the village.

Branch gives Poppy a puzzled look as she runs off. 'Glad I could help,' he mumbles, scratching his head.

Chapter 5

Poppy dances into the village to find Harper and Guy. She sits them down on some soft spotty mushroom stools.

'First I want to thank you for your amazing idea for tomorrow's best ever parade.'

They both look proud.

'Both of you,' Poppy adds.

Guy's face drops. Harper looks shocked. Of course, neither one knew about the other's idea. 'But I have decided on something even more wonderful than what each of you suggested,' she finishes.

Poppy wonders if maybe this isn't quite going right, because they both look awfully disappointed.

'What I mean is: Guy, I'd love it if you could choreograph a dance-a-rific parade to begin at your dance studio and finish at Glitter Falls.'

Guy is overjoyed and emits a fantastic

glitter cloud in his excitement.

Poppy giggles and turns to Harper. Harper looks so gloomy that Poppy gives her a quick hug. 'And, Harper, I'd love it if you could create your papier mâché puppets so that we can build them into the dance!'

Harper's face lights up. 'Really?' she says, her colourful eyes sparkling as she dances from side to side. Harper's hair flicks spots of paint across Poppy's dress that look like cool polka dots and they both laugh.

'Now, down to business,' Poppy says.

'We're going to need the whole village to pull this off, so let's go and find some helpers. But, remember, it must be a surprise for King Peppy.'

So off they go, dancing and singing and swinging through the village. Soon enough, everyone knows what they need to do and they all wait patiently for King Peppy to go to bed for the night. Luckily, Poppy's dear old dad is not a night owl.

As soon as the coast is clear they meet at Guy's dance studio. Karma gives a quiet whistle and a swarm of critters emerge from her hair. The critters make clicking sounds as

their bottoms light up like a string of fabulous fairy lights.

DJ Suki composes some thumping tunes to which Guy can choreograph his dance. Cooper frantically frosts cupcakes and other delicious snacks for everyone in the parade.

Biggie hangs decorations while Satin and Chenille direct. Harper recruits a group of young Trolls to help construct the puppets, while everyone else is in the dance studio learning Guy's awesome moves.

Poppy looks around at her friends and fellow Trolls and feels proud as punch at how they've all pulled together.

Finally, after a hard night's work they fall into their fluffy beds, feeling tired and excited.

Chapter 6

It's early morning on the day of the
parade and Poppy springs out of bed
knowing that today is going to be the
happiest, singing-est, dancing-est,
most hug-filled day in the history of
Troll Village!

She swings out of her pod and heads to
Guy's dance studio. Everyone is outside
and ready to go.

Poppy climbs onto a furry tree stump and rings her cowbell to get the crowd's attention. 'Listen up, everyone,' she says looking around at the crowd. 'This is it! We've all worked our fuzzy butts off to make this day perfect, now it's time to enjoy it. Kick it, DJ Suki!'

Poppy takes her place at the head of the group and DJ Suki gives a long blow from a horn, then the beat kicks in and they're off.

King Peppy is startled by the noise and rushes out of his pod. He is super surprised to see all of his beloved Trolls!

The crowd of Trolls breaks into a loud cheer when they see King Peppy. Soon dancers snake their way past his pod singing and dancing and sending glittery explosions high into the sky. King Peppy swings his hips to the beat. Poppy grins from the other side of the parade.

After the dancers come the papier mâché puppets. They're totally amazing! Each puppet is different and tells the story of King Peppy's life. There is little King Peppy on the day he was born. And King Peppy on his coronation day, followed by him holding baby Poppy in his arms (Poppy's personal favourite!).

Next is heroic King Peppy on the day he led the Trolls to freedom after being held captive by the Bergens. This one gets an especially big cheer from the crowd. King Peppy's eyes are filled with happy, proud tears! He gives Poppy a big double thumbs-up.

The wonderful parade of puppets finishes with King Peppy on the day he passed the crown on to Poppy.

If I wasn't so stinking happy this would totally make me cry, thinks Poppy. *Okay, well maybe I do have a little something in my eye...*

As the last puppet passes by, the Trolls all shout for King Peppy to join them. He leaps from his pod into the crowd, who catch him and pass him along to where he joins Poppy.

The music is pulsing and every Troll in the village moves together, singing and dancing through the forest until they reach Glitter Falls.

As a final surprise, and a very special birthday gift, Poppy unveils a magnificent life-size statue – an exact replica of the papier mâché puppet showing King Peppy leading the Trolls to freedom – that she and Branch had been working on in secret.

This statue will stand beside Glitter Falls as a tribute to King Peppy for all of time.

Once the parade has ended – and the party is just getting started – King Peppy makes his speech. He thanks everyone in the village for making this the happiest, singing-est, dancing-est, proudest day of his life.

Poppy makes a speech too, thanking all the Trolls for their help. 'It wasn't easy to choose between two perfect ideas,' she finishes, 'but Branch helped me remember that bringing friends together is the most perfect idea of all!'

The Trolls cheer and Poppy cheers too. She has always known she can count on her friends, but now she truly believes she can always count on herself, too.

Finally all the cheering calms down and King Peppy puts his arm around Poppy's shoulder. 'What are we waiting for?' he says with a cheeky smile. 'Let's dance!'

BIGGIE and the Big Mix-Up

Scholastic Children's Books,
Euston House, 24 Eversholt Street,
London NW1 1DB, UK

A division of Scholastic Ltd
London ~ New York ~ Toronto ~ Sydney ~ Auckland
Mexico City ~ New Delhi ~ Hong Kong

First published in Australia by Bonnier Publishing, 2017, as two titles:
Poppy and the Parade Problem
Biggie and the Big Mix-Up
This edition published in the UK by Scholastic Ltd, 2018

Poppy and the Parade Problem written by Katie Hewat
Biggie and the Big Mix-Up written by Fiona Harris

ISBN 978 1407 17140 1

Printed and bound in the UK by CPI (Group) Ltd, Croydon, Surrey

2 4 6 8 10 9 7 5 3 1

www.scholastic.co.uk

BIGGIE and the
Big Mix-Up

Trolls

DREAMWORKS

Chapter 1

'Well, Mr Dinkles,' Biggie says to his beloved pet worm. 'It's another Troll-tastic day in Troll Village!'

Biggie cuddles Mr Dinkles to his big blue chest as he looks out of his pod. The sun is sparkling through the trees and happy Trolls of all colours and sizes are swinging past on their brightly coloured hair. They all wave to Biggie as they swing by and he grins

1

and waves back. But today Biggie is looking out for one Troll in particular.

Biggie has invited Branch over for cupcakes and he is due any minute now. Biggie is very excited. He knows that Branch is still getting used to being out of his underground bunker, so Biggie has gone to a lot of effort to make today special. He has even dressed Mr Dinkles in his best top hat and bow tie for the occasion.

'Hey, Branch!' Biggie cries out as he spots Branch zip-lining through the trees towards his pod. 'You're here!'

'Of course I'm here,' Branch snaps, dropping down onto a nearby tree branch. 'You invited me didn't you?'

3

Biggie's smile fades a little. Branch doesn't sound very friendly. Then Biggie remembers that Branch is still practising positivity with Poppy, which makes him feel a bit less upset about Branch's gruff tone.

Biggie thinks that Branch must have remembered what he's learned, too, because he suddenly adds, 'Er, I mean ... thanks for inviting me.'

'My pleasure!' Biggie says, his smile widening. 'Come on in!'

Biggie leads Branch into his pod, and notices him looking at the hundreds of photos of Mr Dinkles everywhere.

4

Biggie is so proud of his photo collection. He has them displayed on the walls, on the mantelpiece and they are completely covering the table. He has even stacked more in mini-piles on the floor!

Everywhere Biggie looks he sees Mr Dinkles, which is just how he likes it!

'Wow,' Branch says. 'You really love taking photos of Mr Dinkles, huh?'

'Yep!' Biggie says, beaming. 'He's so cute! I can't help myself. I'm going to put them all into an album!'

'Really?' Branch mumbles. 'There's an album big enough for all these?'

Biggie isn't sure about the answer. But there is one thing he is sure about. 'Hey, it's cupcake time!' Biggie says brightly. 'You sit down and I'll get them.'

Just as Biggie is reaching into the cupboard he hears a loud yell behind him.

'Aaagghhh!'

Biggie turns to see Branch slip on a pile of photos and fall on to the table. Oh no! The mountain of photos on the

table fly across the room, and Biggie winces as Branch lands with a thump on his bottom. Dozens of photos float gently down, settling all around Branch, some even getting caught in his hair.

'Whoops!' Biggie says, rushing over to pick Branch up off the floor. 'Did you miss the chair?'

'No, I did not miss the chair,' Branch grumbles, picking photos out of his hair. 'I could barely find a chair, and when I did, I slipped on those pictures! What are they doing on the floor? This pod is a health hazard!'

'Oh!' says Biggie feeling very sorry. 'You need a hug, Branch,' he says, leaning over and squeezing the grumpy Troll. 'There – all better. Now it's definitely cupcake time!'

Biggie pops one of the cupcakes into his mouth to make sure it tastes as delicious as it looks. It does.

'You should find a new hobby,' Branch says, rubbing his sore bottom. 'One that isn't so dangerous.'

Biggie feels confused. 'But I love taking photos,' Biggie says quietly.

'I need to get back to my bunker,'

Branch says. 'Where it's safe.' He turns to leave, then Biggie thinks he must remember Poppy's lessons on positivity because he adds, 'Uh ... so ... thanks, Biggie.'

Biggie watches sadly as Branch swings away through the branches still rubbing his bottom. Biggie wonders if Branch could be right. *Does he take too many photos of Mr Dinkles?*

'Mew!' says Mr Dinkles, as if reading Biggie's mind.

Biggie looks down at his pet worm and pushes the thought away. He could never have enough photos of Mr Dinkles. He's so adorable!

A cuddle with Mr Dinkles makes Biggie feel a little better. But he does still feel disappointed. Biggie was so hoping he would share a cupcakes-and-rainbows kind of morning with Branch. Instead, Biggie's guest has swung away without even trying one cupcake, and with a photo of Mr Dinkles still stuck in his hair.

Chapter 2

Biggie decides to clear some photos off the floor of his pod, for the next Troll who pops in to visit. He doesn't want anyone else slipping and ending up with a sore bottom.

As he scoops up a pile of super cute pictures of Mr Dinkles wearing a sparkly green beret, he hears voices outside.

Biggie looks up to see Cooper and DJ Suki swinging from their hair in a nearby tree.

He instantly waves, but they don't see him.

'I hope Biggie has given Mr Dinkles some happy tears for fresh cupcakes,' he hears Cooper say.

'Man, Biggie cries sooooo much,' DJ Suki says. 'No one in Troll Village cries as much as Biggie. I mean...' Biggie strains his ears to hear the rest of what DJ Suki says. He can see that she is still talking but she has swung sideways, so her voice doesn't carry to Biggie's pod.

Biggie sighs. He has heard enough anyway and is feeling very hurt! He was already feeling gloomy after Branch got cross because Biggie has too many photos of Mr Dinkles. Now DJ Suki is saying he cries too much. *Why would DJ Suki say that?* Biggie wonders. *Is crying such a bad thing?*

'Come on, Mr Dinkles,' he says sadly, picking up his beloved pet. 'Let's go and get your new jacket from Satin and Chenille. That'll cheer us up!'

Biggie and Mr Dinkles head off in the opposite direction to Cooper and DJ Suki. Biggie just doesn't want to hear anymore.

13

Satin and Chenille are busy designing their fabulous new jumpsuit when Biggie and Mr Dinkles arrive.

They're so distracted with this latest creation that they don't notice their visitors.

'Girl, this jumpsuit is gonna be super cool!' Biggie hears Satin say.

'You said it,' Chenille agrees. 'Our best yet.'

'Hey, is Mr Dinkle's new jacket ready?' asks Satin.'Yep,' Chenille says. 'I *love* this hipster look for Mr Dinkles. Totally adorable.'

'Uh-huh! That look is *so* in right now,' Satin agrees.

Biggie is thrilled to hear that Mr Dinkles will be such a fashionista. He's about to say so when Satin laughs.

'Biggie and Mr Dinkles may as well be twins like us,' she says. 'Wherever you see Biggie, there's Mr Dinkles too!'

'Yeah,' Chenille giggles. 'Biggie can't even leave his pod without Mr Dinkles!'

16

The twins still don't know Biggie is there and he suddenly doesn't want them to. He quietly slips away feeling even more upset and confused. He thought his friends liked him for who he was. But now he's not so sure. *Do I need to change?* he wonders to himself.

'What if everyone is right, Mr Dinkles?' Biggie whispers, holding the worm tightly to his chest as he walks through Troll Village. 'What if I *do* take too many photos of you? What if I *do* cry too much? What if I *am* too dependent on you?'

'Mew,' says Mr Dinkles sadly. He hates seeing Biggie upset.

17

'I've got it!' Biggie suddenly shouts, making Mr Dinkles jump. 'I need to see Cybil for a good dose of Troll Wisdom!'

Biggie is in such a hurry to get to Cybil's pod that he does something he's never done before and hurries straight past the cupcakery without gobbling a single cupcake.

Chapter 3

Biggie finds Cybil in her pod, suspended by a flying critter gripping her hair while meditating. She opens her eyes when Biggie enters.

'Hello Biggie,' Cybil purrs in her calm voice. 'Is it Hug Time or cupcake time?'

'It's advice time!' Biggie says, placing Mr Dinkles on a nearby cushion.

'How can I help you, Biggie?' Cybil asks. 'Your energy is very chaotic.'

Biggie tells Cybil how confused he is feeling about everything he has overheard.

'So, what do you think?' he asks nervously. 'Do I need to change, Cybil?'

Cybil closes her eyes and breathes deeply. 'Only darkness can bring light,' she says mysteriously.

Cybil's words make Biggie feel even more muddled than he did before. 'Er ... does that mean I should be a

different kind of Troll?' he asks. 'Or that I should have more Glowflies in my pod?'

Cybil opens her eyes and blinks slowly at Biggie. *'Every season passes,'* she says.

'Remember those three words and all will be well.'

Cybil gives Biggie a hug. 'Now, I must continue my meditation,' she says, and the winged critter clutching Cybil's hair flutters towards the ceiling again. 'My chakras need extra attention today.'

Biggie picks up Mr Dinkles, who has been napping peacefully on the cushion.

'Thanks, Cybil. You are very wise.'

As he leaves Cybil's pod, Biggie knows what he must do.

'Of course!' he says to Mr Dinkles as they swing through the trees. '*Every Season Passes* means my season of taking photos, crying happy tears and being so attached to you has passed!'

'Oh, snap!' says Mr Dinkles, not sure he likes what he's hearing.

'I'm going to change my ways!' Biggie says firmly.

'It's time to try new hobbies and
learn some independence. But first,
Poppy's pod!'

Poppy is busy scrapbooking and bedazzling a drawing of Troll Village when Biggie and Mr Dinkles arrive.

'Hey, guys,' she says brightly. 'Grab some glitter and join me for a scrapbooking session.'

'No, thanks, Poppy,' Biggie says in a very deep and serious voice. 'I'm too busy for bedazzling today.'

Poppy looks confused. 'Are you okay, Biggie?' she asks. 'You have NEVER said no to bedazzling. And why are you speaking in that voice? Do you have a cold?'

'This is the way I speak now,' Biggie says in the deep voice again. 'It's the voice of a Troll who would never cry over a lovely sunset or that beautiful drawing you're bedazzling right now.'

'Oookaaay,' Poppy says, still looking confused.

'I've come to ask a favour,' Biggie continues. 'Could you please look after Mr Dinkles for me?'

'Are you going away somewhere?' Poppy asks.

'Only on a journey of self-discovery, Poppy,' Biggie says, handing over

Mr Dinkles to his friend. 'I need to try new things.'

'That's great!' Poppy says, instantly brightening. 'Everyone needs to try new things. Of course I'll look after Mr Dinkles.'

'That would be awesome, thanks Poppy,' Biggie says, hoping he doesn't sound as unsure as he feels. 'See you later.'

Biggie swings away from Poppy's pod, trying desperately to ignore the fact that he is already missing his beloved pet worm.

Chapter 4

The first thing Biggie sees when he gets back to his pod are the photos of Mr Dinkles everywhere. After much collecting, stacking and pushing he manages to squeeze them all into a cupboard.

'There!' he says, forcing the door closed. 'My first step towards a new me.'

He sits down at his newly cleared table to hatch a plan. He has decided to write a list. 'Time to think about new hobbies,' he says. 'Any ideas Mr Dinkles?'

Biggie suddenly remembers that Mr Dinkles is with Poppy. Just the thought of him not being near brings tears to Biggie's eyes, but he quickly blinks them away.

'I'll just have to think of some myself,' he says out loud. 'How hard can it be?'

Biggie's first idea is to try gardening with Karma. He's never gardened before but is sure it will be Troll-tastic!

When he arrives at Karma's greenhouse, she looks more than a little surprised to see Biggie wearing a large-brimmed hat and holding a trowel.

'Hi Karma, I've come to help you garden!' Biggie announces. 'I even brought my own trowel!'

'Oh, that's hair-ific!' says Karma. 'Why don't you start by cutting back those bubblegum-berry bushes?'

'Sure!' Biggie says, excited to help out.

As Karma hands him some pruning shears, Biggie spots three different types of beetles crawling around in

30

Karma's hair. The little critters remind him of Mr Dinkles, so he quickly looks away and heads over to the trees.

Biggie is doing a terrific job cutting back all the twigs with the shears. In fact, he does such a super job and is SO enthusiastic that he accidentally cuts off some bubblegum berries too!

'Er ... those bubblegum berries aren't quite ripe enough to come off yet,' Karma says.

'Whoops, sorry.'

'Maybe you could trim the hedges now?' Karma suggests.

'Good idea!' Biggie agrees.

Biggie enjoys trimming the hedges. As
he works he thinks about how beautiful
the light in Karma's garden is and how
cute Mr Dinkles would look if he were
perched on top of the hedge, especially
if he were wearing...

Biggie stops cutting and looks up to see
Karma behind the hedge watering the
plants. He was so distracted thinking
about Mr Dinkles that he clipped off
the top of Karma's hair!

'Oh! I'm so sorry, Karma,' Biggie says, feeling awful about snipping off some of her lovely green hair.

'That's okay,' Karma says. 'There'll always be more bubblegum berries … and more hair. But maybe you should try a different hobby?'

Biggie is a bit tired of gardening now, and he agrees.

He heads off to Branch's bunker to learn about survival skills.

'What kind of survival skills?' Branch asks. 'Do you want to learn how to

34

cross your pod safely without slipping and breaking your back on those photos?'

'Oh, no!' Biggie says, feeling a bit silly. 'I've put the photos away. My pod is totally safe now.'

'Good to know,' Branch mumbles, rubbing his bottom. 'Well, I can teach you how to build a panic room.'

Biggie nods and tries to look enthusiastic. 'That sounds ... er ... nice.'

'Or how to safety-proof your pod,' Branch continues, looking excited.

35

'I can also show you how to install safety guards and edge-bumpers around your pod so Mr Dinkles can't get hurt...'

'That all sounds ... er ... yeah,' Biggie interrupts, suddenly not so sure this was a good idea. 'But, er, Branch, I might get back to you.'

'Sooner the better,' Branch says firmly. 'A safe pod is a happy pod.'

Biggie hurries away from Branch's bunker.

Survival skills are definitely not for him. Imagine putting Mr Dinkles behind safety guards! What a terrible thought!

The next new hobby on Biggie's list is skateboarding with Aspen. Aspen is happy to have a new thrill-seeking partner. Biggie is a bit wobbly at first but manages to stay upright for most of the time.

'Dude!' Aspen calls as they speed down a steep branch. 'You're coasting!'

Biggie feels chuffed, until the board hits a small stone and he does a triple flip in the air and lands flat on his back.

'Ow!' Biggie says, sitting up and rubbing the back of his head.

'Oh, dude,' says Aspen, coming to help him up. 'Maybe you need something a bit less extreme. Hey look down there, Smidge is about to start her fitness workout!'

'Great idea,' Biggie says. 'Thanks, Aspen.'

'Yippee!' Smidge cries, jumping up and down and clapping her hands when Biggie tells her he wants to join her training session. 'Let's work it!'

Biggie quickly discovers that he's not very good at jumping rope with his own hair, and that weightlifting isn't as easy as he'd thought. He keeps getting pinned down under the heavy barbells. After Smidge lifts the weights off him for the tenth time, she suggests

that maybe Biggie should start with something easier.

'How about you stick to star jumps for now?' she says kindly.

But Biggie is finding star jumps hard, too. Things get even more difficult for Biggie when Smidge plays her Swedish heavy metal music so loudly during the workout! It hurts his ears and makes his tummy feel funny.

He feels like bursting into tears. Sad tears. *This whole being-a-new-kind-of-Troll thing isn't as easy as I thought*, Biggie thinks to himself. But he's determined not to give up!

Chapter 5

After his disastrous workout with
Smidge, Biggie limps back to his pod
feeling sore and lonely. There's no
Mr Dinkles to cuddle, his head is
thumping from the skateboarding
accident and his arms hurt from all the
push-ups Smidge made him do.

Biggie really did his best to enjoy these
new activities, even though his heart
wasn't in it. But he is determined not

to give up. His friends in Troll Village want a new Biggie and that's what they're going to get.

I have to forget about the old Biggie, he thinks, remembering Cybil's wise words. *That season has passed!*

Biggie goes to the cupboard to check for cupcakes, forgetting he crammed all the photos in there earlier. The moment he opens it hundreds of photos fly out, completely covering him. Biggie watches images of Mr Dinkles floating down around him.

Sadness and loneliness suddenly overwhelm Biggie. The big blue Troll

plonks down on the floor in the middle
of all the photos and begins to sob, big
teardrops stream down his cheeks.

Biggie is still crying when he hears loud voices coming from below his pod, in Troll Village. He wipes away his tears and goes to look outside. A bunch of Trolls are gathered in the centre of Troll Village and there's a bit of commotion going on.

Biggie sticks his head out of the pod to try and hear what the Trolls are saying, but they are too far away. All he hears are snippets of their conversations. But one word keeps reaching Biggie's ears again and again. It's his own name!

'Biggie ... photos ... Biggie!' he hears Satin shouting at Poppy.

'Biggie ... no happy tears cupcakes ... Biggie ... biggest supplier...' he hears Cooper shouting to Maddy.

Then Biggie sees Guy Diamond talking to Poppy. Poppy is holding Mr Dinkles and all three of them look upset. The wind carries some of their words up to Biggie's ears.

'Needs something ... not a single mew...'

In that moment Biggie decides enough is enough. He needs to know what is going on down there and what everyone is saying about him. He's tried his hardest to change all day, but if it still isn't enough then he wants

the Trolls to tell him straight to his face!
Most importantly, he needs to know that
Mr Dinkles is okay.

Biggie takes a deep breath and
swings down towards Troll Village
to investigate!

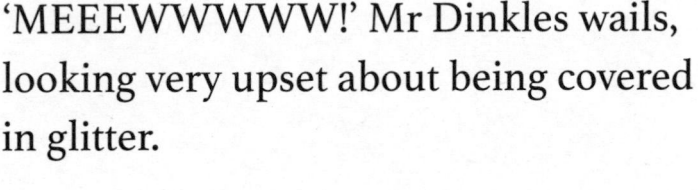

chapter 6

Biggie lands in the middle of Troll Village just in time to hear Guy Diamond say, 'It's Sparkle Time!'

He watches as Guy shakes and glitter falls over Mr Dinkles. 'Ta daaa!' he says proudly. 'Have a glitter day, Mr Dinkles!'

'MEEEWWWWW!' Mr Dinkles wails, looking very upset about being covered in glitter.

48

Biggie runs to his beloved pet. 'Wait!' he cries. 'I'm the one who needed to change, not Mr Dinkles!'

The Trolls all turn to look at him. '*BIGGIE*!'

Biggie stops in his tracks. He stares around in bewilderment as the Trolls surround him and all begin talking at once.

'We can't do our fashion show!' Satin cries.

'I need my happy tear cupcakes!' wails Maddy.

'We can't understand what Mr Dinkles is saying!' says Guy Diamond.

'Wait, wait!' Poppy says, stepping forward. 'One at a time! Satin and Chenille – well, that's two, but – you go first, anyway.'

'We can't even *think* about making another outfit unless you photograph our fashion show, Biggie!' Satin blurts out.

Chenille adds, 'There's no point if you're not there taking your super cool photos!'

51

Biggie is feeling very confused. This was NOT what he was expecting to hear.

Then Poppy holds out a mewing Mr Dinkles to Biggie and his heart melts.

'And Mr Dinkles needs you to give him a hug,' Poppy says. 'He's been trying to tell us something and we think it's that he really misses you!'

Biggie rushes forward to take Mr Dinkles. The worm immediately stops mewing and snuggles close to his best pal. Biggie feels a million times better with Mr Dinkles back in his arms and a huge smile spreads across his face.

'We miss seeing you and Mr Dinkles together,' adds Guy Diamond.

'But I heard Satin and Chenille talking about how I couldn't leave my pod without him,' Biggie says, clutching the worm tight to his chest. 'They thought I was too dependent on him.'

'Whaaaat?' Satin cries. 'Nu-uh! You can still be independent even if you're not alone!'

'Yeah, and we should know,' Chenille says, winking at her sister. 'Isn't that right, girl?'

'You know it!' Satin says, high-fiving her twin.

'Troll Village just isn't the same without you and Mr Dinkles,' Branch says.

'Really?' Biggie says in surprise.

'Also, your photos are great,' Branch continues sincerely. 'You should take as many photos of Mr Dinkles as you want.'

'You are definitely getting the hang of this positivity thing,' a smiling Poppy says to Branch.

'More importantly, can you PLEASE

start making happy tears again?' Cooper begs. 'Troll Village isn't the same without Biggie's happy tears cupcakes!'

'But I heard DJ Suki saying I cry too much,' Biggie says.

'Hang on,' DJ Suki says. 'I did say that but I also said that you cry so much because you are special and appreciate the important things in Troll life!'

'Oh, I didn't hear that bit,' Biggie admits. 'I thought my season of crying and taking photos had passed.'

'Dear, sweet Biggie,' Cybil says, floating towards him. '*Every Season Passes* meant

55

that your sad feelings would soon go away.'

'But I thought you all wanted me to change,' Biggie says, feeling more confused than ever. 'I thought everyone wanted me to be a different Troll.'

'Oh Biggie,' Poppy says, smiling and shaking her head. 'Don't you know that you are a unique Troll, and that we love you exactly as you are?'

Biggie looks around at Poppy and all his friends. It feels as if one of Smidge's barbells is being lifted off his shoulders. Everyone loves him for the Troll he is and there's no need to

change a single thing about himself!
Just knowing this makes him feel like
the happiest Troll in the whole village.

The Trolls all gather around Biggie in a giant group hug and he cries a waterfall of happy tears.

'Looks like it's cupcake time!' Biggie sobs happily and everyone gives a huge cheer.

That night, Biggie and Mr Dinkles sit in the front row of Satin and Chenille's awesome fashion show and Biggie takes loads of photos. Poppy hands around a fresh batch of happy tears cupcakes as the crowd of Trolls 'Ooh' and 'Aah' over the twins' fabulous new jumpsuit.

Everyone seems to be thrilled that Biggie is himself again and that all is back to normal in Troll Village. But no Troll could be more thrilled than Biggie himself.

Biggie now knows that he is being true to himself, which means that everything will be cupcakes and rainbows from now on!

Flip me over for the next story!

Hug Time!

Flip me over for the next story!